WATERSHIP™ DOWN

Pipkin Makes a Friend

Diane Redmond

RED FOX

A Red Fox Book

Published by Random House Children's Books
20 Vauxhall Bridge Road, London SW1V 2SA

A division of The Random House Group Ltd
London Melbourne Sydney Auckland
Johannesburg and agencies throughout the world

www.watershipdown.net

Illustrations by County Studio, Leicester

1 3 5 7 9 10 8 6 4 2

Printed and bound in Italy by Lego SPA

THE RANDOM HOUSE GROUP Limited Reg. No. 954009

www.randomhouse.co.uk

ISBN 0 09 940325 0

This story represents scenes from the television series, Watership Down,
which is inspired by Richard Adams' novel of the same name.

The rabbits hopped into the bean field and
quickly took cover under the big, floppy leaves.

'This looks like a safe place to rest,' said Hazel.

'Good – I'm worn out,' groaned Hawkbit.

While the bigger rabbits settled down for
a nap, Pipkin hopped off after a toad.

'Don't go too far,' warned Hazel.

At the edge of the field Pipkin saw a big gull sitting on a fence post. 'Hello,' he said.

'Waah!' squawked the gull. 'You give Kehaar big fright!'

Pipkin giggled. 'Where are you from?' he asked.

'Big water – full of fish,' said Kehaar. 'You know where is big water?' he asked hopefully.

Pipkin shook his head. 'No, we're lost, too.'

'Hungry. Want fish,' wailed the gull, and flew away.

Pipkin hopped back to his friends, who were getting ready to leave. There were dark clouds everywhere and a cold wind was blowing.

'We must go now – before the storm breaks,' urged Hazel.

They carried on until they came to a peat bog.

'We can't cross that!' said Dandelion.

'Well it's not safe to stop here,' said Hazel.

As the rabbits struggled across the bog, sharp thorns stuck to their fur.

'I've had enough,' said Hawkbit. 'We've been looking for Fiver's high hills for days – and now this!'

'I don't think Fiver knows where we're going,' said Dandelion. 'We should go back to the old warren.'

'Nobody's going anywhere,' growled Bigwig, the biggest rabbit in the group. 'Now hop to it.'

They moved on, but Bigwig whispered to Hazel, 'What if Fiver's wrong? We can't keep going on dreams.'

'Why not?' sighed Hazel. 'They're all we have left.'

As evening approached, the rabbits were crossing a moor,
where a light mist had gathered. Fiver was tired and hungry.
He tripped and landed in a puddle, where he sat shivering.
'Come on,' said Hazel. 'The high hills can't be far now.'

'I'm scared there won't be any high hills,' said Fiver.

'Don't say that – you saw them!' Hazel reminded him.

'Yes, in a dream,' said Fiver.

Hazel smiled. 'If we stop believing, we're lost.'

Suddenly Bigwig stopped. 'Hazel,' he gasped, pointing straight ahead. 'Come here!'

The mist had cleared and a shaft of sunlight shone down on a faraway group of hills.

'Fiver!' said Hazel. 'Look! The high hills!'

Fiver gazed at the distant landscape. 'They're real,' he cried. 'Hazel, the hills are real!'

Hawkbit and Dandelion looked on happily.

'You were right, lad,' said Bigwig. 'You were right all along.'

Close by there was a small farm with a barn, paddocks and a vegetable garden.

'Mmm!' said Blackberry. 'I can smell cabbage.'

'I'm starving,' said Hawkbit.

'I could run to the high hills on a belly full of carrots,' laughed Bigwig. 'What are we waiting for?'

'Just a minute,' warned Hazel. 'There may be dogs or cats or Man down there.'

'I don't care – I want some lettuce!' said Dandelion.

'At least wait until dusk,' Hazel suggested. 'It'll be safer.'

Bigwig nodded. 'All right,' he said.

Later, as the rabbits crept into the vegetable garden,
a mouse scampered into the tractor shed.

Kehaar swooped down and landed beside the mouse.
'Hello, Hannah! Want fish!'

Hannah stared at the bird. 'You can't keep stealing
the farm cat's fish,' she said.

The gull squawked sadly. 'Kehaar hungry!'

Hannah sighed. 'Follow me. But this is the last time.'

The cat's bowl was full of sardines.

'Quick, eat!' the mouse whispered. 'The cat's not here.'

But the cat *was* there. She was sitting on the tractor.
Her tail flicked crossly. With a leap, she sprang
through the air and landed on Kehaar. 'Rraw!' she
spat furiously.

When the rabbits heard the cat they ran out of the vegetable garden and bolted across the farmyard.

As they passed the shed, Pipkin ran slap-bang into Hannah.

'Run! Run!' she told him. 'The cat's got Kehaar.'

'Kehaar?' said Pipkin. 'He's my friend, I must help him.'

And the young rabbit hopped into the shed.

'Pipkin!' cried Hazel. 'Come back!'

Inside the shed, Kehaar was putting up a brave fight.

'Come on,' he said. 'I not frightened.'

The cat slashed at the gull and drew blood from his wing.

'Caaaw!' Kehaar cried in pain.

Bigwig, Hazel and Hawkbit, who were watching from the
entrance of the shed, charged at the cat.

'Yowl!' she howled, as she went flying through the air and
landed with a crash underneath a pile of flowerpots.

'Are you badly hurt?' Pipkin asked Kehaar.

'Not bad,' said Kehaar. 'Maybe not fly so good for a while.'

'Then come with us to the high hills,' said Pipkin. 'You'll be safe there.'

'Now hang on a minute,' said Bigwig crossly.

'He's a friend,' Pipkin begged. 'Please.'

Hazel looked at the wounded gull and the tired mouse. 'We're all newcomers here,' he said. 'We need to help each other.' He looked at his friends, who were all nodding.

Slowly, Bigwig nodded his head too. 'All right,' he said. 'Now, let's get going!'

Led by Kehaar, who flew low beside them with Hannah on his back, the rabbits travelled through the night. Finally, at dawn, they reached the foot of the high hills.

'They're big!' gasped Hawkbit, pulling himself up the steep bank.

'We're nearly there,' said Hazel.

After a while, the rabbits reached the top of the hill, where a soft breeze cooled their hot faces.

Fiver smiled as he gazed around. 'This is the place, Hazel!' he cried. 'This is where we'll begin again.'

'It's called Watership Down,' said Hannah.

'Watership Down,' whispered Fiver. 'Home.'